"Eligible means you have to be eight fairy years old to go to the ball," said Goldie. "And you are not eight."

"I *am* eight," said Sylva. "Or I will be eight very soon. On Saturday."

"Yes, that's true," said Rosy gently. "But the ball is on Friday, and your birthday is the next day, Sylva. You'll still be seven on Friday night when the ball is held. So you'll have to wait till next year to go to your first ball."

"No!" cried Sylva. "That's not fair!"

"Better luck next year!" said Goldie.

"*Squeak!*" cried Squeak.

Sylva flew to her room and cried and cried. Not go to the ball! Impossible!

THE
fairy bell
SISTERS

Sylva
and the
Fairy Ball

Margaret McNamara

ILLUSTRATIONS BY JULIA DENOS

BALZER + BRAY
An Imprint of HarperCollinsPublishers

In the spirit of J. M. Barrie, who created Peter Pan
and Tinker Bell, the author has donated a portion of
the proceeds from the sale of this book to the
Great Ormond Street Hospital.

Balzer + Bray is an imprint of HarperCollins Publishers.

Sylva and the Fairy Ball
Text copyright © 2013 by Margaret McNamara
Illustrations copyright © 2013 by Julia Denos

Library of Congress Cataloging-in-Publication Data
McNamara, Margaret.
  Sylva and the Fairy Ball / Margaret McNamara ; illustrations by Julia Denos.
— 1st ed.
  p. cm. — (The fairy Bell sisters)
  Summary: Sylva Bell is not old enough to attend the Fairy Ball with her sisters Clara, Rosy, and Golden, but when a horde of trolls crashes the ball, Sylva bravely comes to the rescue.
  ISBN 978-0-06-222802-4 (hardcover bdg.) — ISBN 978-0-06-222801-7 (pbk. bdg.)
  [1. Fairies—Fiction. 2. Sisters—Fiction. 3. Balls (Parties)—Fiction. 4. Courage—Fiction.] I. Denos, Julia, ill. II. Title.
PZ7.M47879343Syl 2013   2012024990
[Fic]—dc23   CIP
                                                                          AC

Typography by Erin Fitzsimmons
13 14 15 16 17 CG/OPM 10 9 8 7 6 5 4 3
❖
First Edition

for
Betsy Morrell

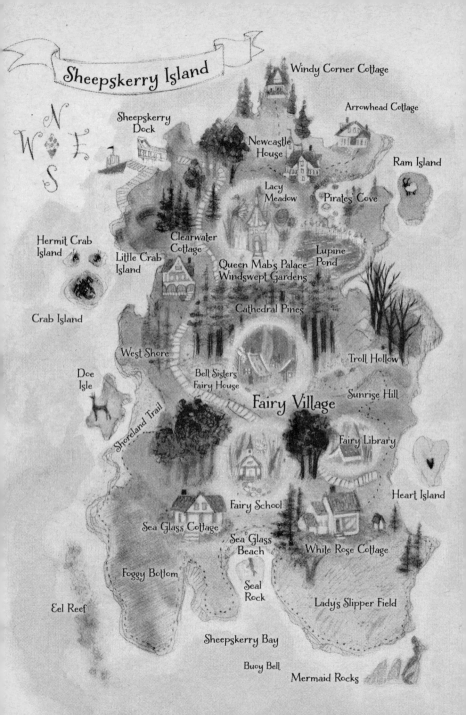

THE
fairy bell
SISTERS

one

Everybody has heard of the Fairy Ball on Sheepskerry Island, for it's the only ball where fairies put on their diamond wings and walk on satin ribbons under the stars. But only a few of us will ever see those diamonds or find those ribbons. This is what they look like, just so you'll know when you do see them.

And though this is quite a secret, I'll tell you something as long as you promise not to tell anyone else: This year's ball was nearly ruined. And it would have been, except for one of Tinker Bell's little sisters.

Oh yes, of *course* Tinker Bell has little sisters. Tink is a grown-up fairy, so she lives on the island of Neverland with her friend Peter Pan. Some people think Tink's entire family lives in Kensington Gardens in London, as that's where Tink was born, but that's not true at all. Her little sisters aren't grown up yet, so their home is with the younger fairies on Sheepskerry Island, which I believe is not far from where you are right now. You may have been there without even knowing it, as on maps used by grown-up people it goes by another name. But perhaps you'll recognize it if I describe it to you. It's a jewel of a place, bright green in spring, silent white in winter, filled with sturdy yellow roses in summer and flaming leaves in autumn. And it holds all manner of secret things that you will know about very soon. If you read the next chapter, that is.

two

But I am forgetting my manners. Have you met Tinker Bell's little sisters? Please allow me to introduce them. May I present:

Clara Bell   Rosy Bell

Golden Bell   Sylva Bell

and baby Squeak

Clara Bell, Rosy Bell, Golden Bell, Sylva Bell, and baby Squeak live with the other young fairies on Sheepskerry Island. There are no sheep on Sheepskerry anymore, which is a good thing, as sheep are enormous monsters of preposterous size, as everyone knows. (Actually, Tinker Bell's little sisters only know about sheep from the stories they've heard from their fairy godmother, Queen Mab, the most powerful fairy of all.)

Tinker Bell's little sisters go to fairy school,

and eat fairy food,

and play fairy games,

and stay away from trolls,

and once a year,

they go to a Fairy Ball,

if they are old enough.

Which, this year, Sylva Bell was not.

Do you suppose Sylva Bell wanted to go with her sisters to the ball? Oh yes, she did. She wanted to go so much that she did something very, very naughty. Something you would never do, I feel quite sure, even if you meant well, as Sylva did. Sylva made such a mess of things the day before the Fairy Ball that I'm not even sure I should tell you about it.

I'll leave the choice to you. If you would like to hear about perfect little fairies and the perfect things they do, please go find another book.

If you would like to hear about a brave little fairy who can also be rather naughty and get in *very* big trouble with her sisters, just turn the page.

three

O h, thank goodness
you turned the page!

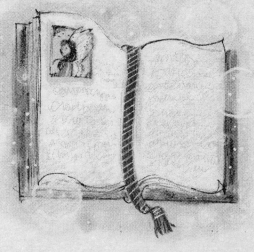

four

That summer, Sylva Bell was seven fairy years old. Fairy years are different from our years, so it is a long, long time between birthdays. That is why fairies look forward to their birthdays so very much.

"What sort of cake would you like this year, Sylva?" asked Rosy. The sisters were in the garden behind their fairy house, fetching water from Deepwater Spring.

"I think Sylva should have a carrot cake," said Clara. "Carrot cakes can be quite healthful for a fairy."

"Better for a rabbit," said Goldie. "Right,

Squeakie?"

Squeak squeaked.

Sylva flew over to the handle and started pumping.

"Hold on, Sylva!" said Clara. "You need to prime it first."

If you haven't pumped springwater recently, you might have forgotten, as Sylva had, that the pump must be primed to get the water flowing. The sisters always left a small jug of water near the pump for that very purpose. "This will start things up," said Clara.

Sylva pumped the creaky handle up and down, up and down. The water gurgled, sputtered, and then came out in a gush.

"It's freezing!" Sylva laughed.

"Mind my shoes!" said Goldie. She had painted them herself, and she was very fond of them.

"If I were Sylva," said Rosy, carefully filling their water jugs, one at a time, "I think I would

like to make my own choice of birthday cake."

"I *would* like to make my own choice," Sylva said. Cakes, of course, were the Bakewell sisters' specialty. Sylva remembered the splendid cake she had had at their fairy house last summer. "Could we have a blueberry cake?" she asked.

"Coomada, coomada!" said Squeak.

"Yes, you love berries, don't you?" said Rosy, sweeping up baby Squeak in her arms. Squeak had a language all her own, which her sisters understood.

Clara, Rosy, Goldie, and Sylva headed back to the house with their jugs of water. It was hard work.

"I won't mind being grown up so we can just magic water whenever we want," said Goldie. "How heavy these are!"

Sylva was still thinking about her birthday cake. "Could we make a practice cake today, do you think?" she asked, and Rosy smiled. "There are one or two bushes where the blueberries are already ripe."

"Not down near Troll Hollow, I hope," said Clara gravely.

"Not too close by," said Rosy. She shivered. "I stay very clear of Troll Hollow and the awful trolls who live there."

They all thought about the trolls and their terrible mischief for a moment. "No, the berries are on the east side of Sunrise Hill. We'll be fine there."

"I'd go with you," said Goldie. "But I might catch my wings on the bushes."

"My wings are not as delicate as yours," said Rosy. "So I don't mind going."

"Carrot cake would be more practical," Clara said.

But Rosy was already off, with Squeak in one arm and an empty acorn cap in the other, to pick berries for her sister.

five

Once the water jugs were in the pantry and covered with tea towels, Clara put some wood in the oven to get it hot.

"Normally I'd let Goldie mix the batter," said Clara, "as she's the third oldest. But she must be out looking for sea glass again."

"I'll do it," said Sylva.

"All right," said Clara, "you can do it. If you pay attention and follow the recipe."

"I'm not looking for sea glass," called Goldie from upstairs. "I'm trying on my gown for the Fairy Ball."

"The Fairy Ball?" cried Sylva. "Why didn't you tell me?"

"Queen Mab hasn't even set a date for the ball yet, Sylva." Clara shook her head. "Goldie just likes any excuse to try on her ball gowns."

"I heard that!" said Goldie. She came to the top of the stairs in a tiered chiffon skirt and a blouse with matching ruffles. She'd topped the whole outfit with a flowing tartan coat.

"I don't know how you do it, Goldie,"

said Clara. "On anyone else that would look ridiculous."

"Rosy says you have flair," said Sylva.

"I know! I do!" said Goldie.

Clara heaved a long sigh. "It gets so chilly at night, Goldie. You won't be wearing that flimsy gown if the ball is held in late summer."

"I've heard it won't be," sang Goldie, and she flew off to put together another creation.

"I'm definitely going this year," said Sylva. "I'll be eight years old in one little week! Queen Mab will have to let me in."

"If you are eight years old at the time of the ball, then of course you will go," said Clara. "But not a moment before."

Sylva sifted the flour into a fragile pile.

"I love this part," she said.

"Look—you've gotten it all over the table," said Clara, as she creamed the butter and sugar. "Sweep that up, please."

Sylva swept it up, though most of it got on the floor.

"Now for the eggs, Sylva," she said. "Just give me a minute to butter the pan. I really should have done that before we started." She wiped her hands on her apron. "Then I'll watch as you crack."

If Clara had thought about it, she would have known that it's pretty hard to ask someone to wait to crack an egg, especially if that someone is Sylva. Clara might have mentioned, too, that Sylva should have checked the recipe before she took the next step. Or asked someone to help.

But Goldie was busy upstairs.

And Rosy was still out with Squeak.

And Clara didn't remind Sylva to follow the directions.

And Sylva didn't follow the directions.

Crack.

Crack.

If you think Sylva smashed the eggs against the bowl and filled the batter with shells . . . you are only partially right. What she also didn't remember was—

"Not like that!" cried Clara.

Six

The cake turned out fine.

"I think it's better blueberry cake than the Bakewell sisters make," said Rosy. "Even if you didn't separate the eggs."

"Or whip the whites and fold them in," said Clara, "the way the recipe says to."

"I'm not sure I like the crunchiness," said Goldie.

"Eggshells are full of goodness," said Rosy, though she did not sound too convincing.

There was a knock at the door.

"Snail mail!" cried Goldie. The Mail Snail carried a creamy white envelope in its pouch.

"Ooh! It's from Queen Mab, just as I told you. Read it, Clara!"

The envelope was addressed to the Fairy Bell sisters. They opened it together. Inside was an invitation.

Every eligible fairy
on Sheepskerry Island
is invited to the Fairy Ball
this Friday night,
at Queen Mab's palace
in the Windswept Gardens.
There will be cupcakes and ice cream,
a petting zoo,
dancing,
games with prizes,
and presents.

Diamond wings
will be worn.

Sylva was so excited! Her first ball! She'd finally hear Queen Mab's insect orchestra. She'd walk on satin ribbons to get to the fairy palace. She'd pet the queen's own little pony and cradle her magic white mice. She'd eat as many cupcakes as she wanted. And open presents. And stay up late, dancing till dawn.

There was just one thing that puzzled her.

"What does 'eligible' mean?" she asked her sister Clara. Clara was bouncing Squeak on her knee, to Squeak's utter delight.

"Apa!" said Squeak.

"Oh, you want *more*, do you?" said Clara.

But before Clara could answer Sylva's question, Goldie cut in.

"Eligible means you have to be eight fairy years old to go to the ball," said Goldie. "And you are not eight."

"I *am* eight," said Sylva. "Or I will be eight very soon. On Saturday."

"Yes, that's true," said Rosy gently. "But the ball is on Friday, and your birthday is the next day, Sylva. You'll still be seven on Friday night when the ball is held. So you'll have to wait till next year to go to your first ball."

"No!" cried Sylva. "That's not fair!"

"Better luck next year!" said Goldie.

"*Squeak!*" cried Squeak.

Sylva flew to her room and cried and cried. Not go to the ball! Impossible!

Seven

But it was possible. In fact, it was true. Sylva Bell was not allowed to go to the ball. It was the Fairy Way. Sylva Bell was so sad she cried fairy tears that covered the evening flowers with morning-time dew. Even Squeak tugging at her skirt and saying, "No lolo," did not make her feel any better.

"What do you mean, 'Don't be sad'?" Sylva replied to Squeak, rather crossly. "You'd be sad, too, if you were one day too young to go to the ball."

On Tuesday morning, Sylva did not even have fairy breakfast with her sisters. And this was a particular sacrifice on her part, because Tuesday fairy breakfasts are utterly delicious: lingonberry jam and wheat-berry toast; pomegranate juice poured over fresh-cut peaches; sweet oatmeal with sultanas and apples; blue hen eggs, medium-boiled; and prunes. Plus, that Tuesday, there was leftover blueberry cake.

"Apa!" said Squeak.

"Here's some more," said Sylva as she popped some cake crumbs into Squeak's mouth. "But Clara will take care of you today. I'm afraid I need to go out for a while."

Sylva flew sadly amid the fairy houses to the tip of Cathedral Pines, right at the top of Sheepskerry Island. She usually felt better there, for the pines were very high, and when the mist was rising, the sunlight streamed through the branches and made the whole thing look just like a dream. But today, even the chittering of the brown squirrels and the sweet, far-off whistles of the ospreys did not cheer her up. She sat down on the moss and sighed.

Just then Sylva's best friend, Poppy Flower, flew up and landed lightly next to her. Poppy wrapped an arm around Sylva.

"I just heard!" said Poppy. "I am so sorry you can't go to the ball, Sylva. You must feel dreadful!" She gave Sylva a tight hug.

Sylva just sniffed.

"It's so unfair!" said Poppy. "To miss it by one day!"

"I know!"

"I'm not going to the ball either. I'm still too young."

"Your birthday is ages away," said Sylva. "Mine's soon. But not soon enough."

"Yes. That's true. It makes it so much worse for you." Poppy was a very good friend.

"It does!" said Sylva. "Maybe I could sneak in—just for a bit! No one would see me. I so long to see those diamond wings."

"Sylva! You wouldn't! Sneaking into the Fairy Ball would be a terrible thing to do. What would Queen Mab say?"

Sylva didn't want to think.

"I won't do anything like that," said Sylva. "Not really."

"Of course you won't." Poppy looked over at

Sylva. "Promise?" she said.

"Promise," said Sylva.

If only Sylva had not had to break her promise!

eight

That afternoon was spent in lessons (Magic, Flying at Night, Troll Tracks), and so it went by pretty quickly. Sylva was feeling a bit better just before suppertime that evening. Then Clara said, "Supper will be a

little late tonight, Sylva, I'm sorry to say."

"Oh, that's right!" said Goldie. "We have an extra lesson." She sighed. "Poor us."

"That's too bad," said Sylva. "What is it? Not Fairy Dishwashing, I hope!" Fairy Dishwashing was a subject Sylva always tried to avoid.

"No," said Clara. "An extra dancing lesson. The Grace sisters say they'll tie pebbles on our wings and have us waltz around that way."

"Pebbles on your wings?" said Sylva. "Why would they do that?"

"At the ball, our wings will be heavier," said Rosy gently, "so the Graces want us to practice. The lesson is called Dancing with Diamond Wings."

Well, if you were Sylva you would have done the same. She spun in the air and flew off without another word.

"You only have to wait another year!" Goldie called after her.

"Hush, Golden Bell," said Rosy. "Don't make it harder for her."

"Oh, she doesn't mind," said Goldie.

But Sylva minded. She minded very much indeed.

nine

Wednesday at the Bell fairy house was spent in Fairy Ball preparation, and there was more of the same the day after. Sylva could take no more of choosing between curly hair or straight, coral bangles or shell cuffs, silk wraps or satin. Luckily, Poppy stopped by the morning before the ball and took Sylva by the hand.

"Come on, Sylva, let's see what we can find on the beach today," said Poppy.

And so the two best friends went for a long walk on the Shoreland Trail. The beach was beautiful that day; cool and empty, it belonged

to the sea alone. As they walked and Sylva felt
the sand under her feet and looked out at the
wild white waves, her troubles began to fall
away. The water can do that for a fairy.

Sylva thought about going to the ball next
year. She began to picture herself in a gown of
forest green, to match her name. "I'll put shells

in my hair, Poppy, and sea glass on my dancing slippers. I'll twirl and spin and everyone will say what a lovely young fairy I am. Ooh, and maybe Tink will even come see me at my first ball."

"I'm sure she will, Sylva," said Poppy, though she was fairly sure Tink would do nothing of the kind.

"And you'll look nice, too," said Sylva.

"Of course I will," said Poppy. "And we'll have diamond wings."

"Clara says that the diamond wings are made of moonglow, and it's only the Narwhal's Tusk that turns the glow into jewels. The Narwhal's Tusk must be really magical."

"It's the strongest magic on Sheepskerry Island. Maybe even in the Wide World."

"That's why Queen Mab takes it out just once a year at the Fairy Ball."

They both thought about that for a while. Next year did not seem so very far away anymore, and that cheered them up a lot.

"Let's collect some decorations for Clara and Rosy and Goldie," said Sylva. "They might like shells for their hair—"

"I'm not sure, Sylva. . . ."

"—and starfish for their dancing shoes."

"Haven't they chosen all their own decorations already? Goldie must know just what she's wearing."

"Of course she does, but I know I would like it if someone did such a thing for me!"

Poppy wasn't so sure, but the two best friends scoured the Shoreland Trail for all manner of treasure.

They found three hermit crabs, two of whom agreed to act as shoe buckles for one night. They collected heaps of sea glass, some of it the rarest shade of deep blue. And the mermaids, usually so greedy, took pity on the two little fairies and gave them a bucket filled with ropes of tiny seed pearls. "And you don't even have to bring them back," they sang.

The sun was going down by the time Poppy and Sylva had finished their treasure hunt.

"Come on, Poppy! Let's get home before dark so we can show my big sisters what we've done for them!"

ten

It took Sylva a long time to get home because she was so laden down with treasure for her sisters. Clara, Rosy, Golden, and Squeak were all asleep by the time Sylva walked through the birch-twig door.

The great room was pitch-dark, so Sylva lit a fairy lantern. What she saw took her breath away.

Three gowns were hung on the mantelpiece. Three pairs of dancing pumps and three little evening bags were set next to the dresses. Set out on the dressing table were sparkling necklaces, and a pile of earrings, bracelets, and rings.

And tiaras! Never had she seen anything so utterly gorgeous.

Sylva's gaze lingered over the lovely dresses and shoes and jewels. She knew it was naughty not to ask her sisters' permission before she started changing their outfits and adding to their dresses. But she didn't want to wake them up. They had such a big day ahead of them!

"I'll be quick and careful," she said to herself. "They'll be so happy in the morning!"

Sylva turned to Clara's dress, which suited Clara perfectly: It seemed very simple at first, but she could see it was beautifully made, with lots of hidden tucks and delicate bell sleeves. *Perfect for a Fairy Bell sister,* Sylva thought. Clara's dark skin made her look beautiful in vibrant color. She had chosen a deep turquoise silk with beads on the neckline and hem.

What would Clara like best? She rummaged through her bucket of shells as quietly as she could. Even so, they seemed to make a great rumbling sound. Sylva stopped rummaging. The rumbling went on for a moment; then it stopped.

"*Squeak!*" said Squeak, standing up in her crib, which was placed, as are all fairy cribs, in a cozy nook of the great room.

"Oh, it was you making that noise!" said Sylva. "Squeak, you did startle me."

Sylva picked up baby Squeak, checked her fairy diaper (luckily not wet!), and brought her over to help. Then she heard another rumble. Very faint, very distant. Squeak squeaked again, more quietly this time.

"Hush, now," said Sylva. "Not to worry about that racket. I'm sure it's nothing at all."

eleven

You've guessed it, I'll wager. The racket Sylva heard was not made by baby Squeak at all.

But let's not speak of trolls now, while everything's going so nicely. Surely the trolls wouldn't be getting up to too much mischief. Not on the eve of the Fairy Ball.

twelve

All night long, Sylva worked hard. She had to move the jewelry off the dressing table so she could use it to do her work. "I'll put it all back, Squeak, don't worry."

Sylva knew just what would suit Clara's outfit best. She sewed six bright pieces of sea glass on the neckline of Clara's turquoise gown.

"Doo!" said Squeak.

"Oh, do you think it's pretty?" asked Sylva. She sewed on two more.

"A-dah!" said Squeak.

"Yes, I'd say it's perfect, too."

Next, Sylva looked at Rosy's cheerful pink

gingham dress a long time. It was fresh and sweet and not too fancy, just like Rosy.

"Rosy doesn't think she's as pretty as other fairies," Sylva whispered to Squeak. "But I think she's the loveliest of them all."

Sylva wanted to do a good job for Rosy. She was planning to save the hermit crabs for Golden, but she noticed that they both had a little pink sheen to their shells, so she tied them onto Rosy's dancing shoes. It was fiddly work, as the hermit crabs weren't used to being shoe buckles, and they were rather snappish.

When it came to Goldie's dress, Sylva knew she'd have to get it just right.

Golden's dress quite took her breath away. It was pure white, whiter than the snow just after it falls. The top would show off Goldie's pretty shoulders. And the skirt! Well, it was made of the softest down feathers and looked as if it could float away.

"This will be so beautiful when Goldie gets her diamond wings!" said Sylva in a hushed voice. "What could I possibly do to make it more beautiful still?"

thirteen

Sylva carefully chose her most precious items for Goldie: the ropes of seed pearls the mermaids had given her. She had thought she might save them for Tinker Bell's homecoming, but Tinker Bell so rarely came home these days that it seemed a shame not to use them for Golden's gown.

Sylva knew she would have to be very, very careful with Golden's gown. It was so delicate and precious. But slowly, painstakingly, Sylva sewed on the ropes of pearls. At first it went pretty well, and the pearls sat easily on the downy feathers. But Sylva was so tired, and

her hand was shaking because she was worried she wouldn't do it *just* right, and soon things went a bit wrong. A few of the downy feathers got crushed under the weight of the pearls. A few more disappeared as Sylva snipped here and there to make everything even. And then snipped again to get it just right. Sylva's eyelids were heavy, which made it hard for her to concentrate. Finally she cut off the last thread. It was almost dawn.

"All done, Squeak," she said. But Squeak had

fallen asleep hours ago. Sylva looked around the great room. It was a dreadful mess, she had to admit. But there would be time enough to tidy everything up. Her sisters wouldn't be awake for hours.

Sylva lifted up Golden's dress and held it to her in front of the fairy mirror. "I *think* this will be perfect for Goldie," she said to herself. "But there's only one way to be sure."

Gently, oh so gently, Sylva picked up Golden's gown.

"I know I really shouldn't," she whispered to Squeak. "But it's the only way to make sure I've done a good enough job for Goldie." Sylva lifted the dress up into the air and slipped it over her head. Then she turned around to look in the mirror and—

"Sylva! What are you doing?" Goldie's panicked voice pierced the silence of the dawn. "My dress! You've ruined my dress!"

"No, no, Goldie! I was just trying—"

"You spiteful little busybody! Get that off right now!"

"Goldie, I—"

"Get it OFF!"

I'm sure you have guessed what Sylva did not. Goldie, who usually loved to sleep in late, had been awakened by the excitement of the ball. She had come downstairs to try on her dress one more time. And what had she found?

"It's a disaster in here! Sylva, you are in *so much trouble!*"

Sylva's tears fell on the silk. She was trying to be so good. Couldn't she make Golden understand?

"Stop that crying! You'll ruin it even more!"

"*What* is going on?" Clara, in her flannel pajamas, peered down into the great room. She looked around at the scene.

Goldie stood as still as a statue, her hands on

her hips, her cheeks flaming. Snippets of fabric and thread were caught in the fairy carpet of moss on the floor. Shells, seaweed, driftwood, and yes, even sand, were scattered everywhere. Rosy's gown was in a crumpled heap, one of the hermit crabs had wandered away, and three of Clara's new sea-glass jewels were already falling off. The commotion had woken up Squeak and made her wail. And in the corner of the room, Sylva, half-in, half-out of Goldie's gown, was racked with sobs.

"Sylva! What have you done? Here, let me help you." Clara glided down to poor Sylva and helped her struggle out of the gown, which was sadly drooping under the weight of the mermaids' pearls.

"Look at my dress! It's ruined!"

Clara flew over to Squeak to calm her down. "I'm sure Sylva has an explanation for this," Clara said sternly. Then she saw her tiara and bracelets spilled on the floor. "Sylva! Did you do this?"

"I didn't think that—"

"No, you didn't think, did you?" said Clara.

"You were trying to ruin the Fairy Ball for us because you're too young to go!"

"Golden!" Rosy's voice rang out as she came down the stairs. "That is too, too unkind of you. I'm sure Sylva was only—"

But then Rosy caught sight of her own pink dress in a heap on the floor. Her breath caught in her throat. "Oh, Sylva," she said, "what have you done?"

"Please, no, Rosy," said Sylva in a whisper. "Not you, too."

And, as the morning sun streamed through the windows, Sylva ran up to her fairy bedroom and cried and cried and cried.

fourteen

The chilly mood that had descended over Tinker Bell's little sisters was barely warmed by evening, when it was time to go to the ball. Sylva had spent the day asleep, which was just as well, for none of her sisters wanted to see her very much. They had thought they'd enjoy the morning with their fairy friends, curling their hair around pinecones and painting their nails with elderberry polish, but instead they found themselves cleaning up Sylva's mess and repairing their gowns.

"I quite like the idea of hermit crabs on my shoes," said Rosy. "If only they'd keep still. And

Sylva's sea glass is pretty on your dress, Clara, don't you think?"

"She did do a nice job with that," said Clara. "But they weren't sewn on tight enough. That's why they fell off. Poor Sylva! Trying to do so much in just one night."

"'Poor Sylva' nothing!" said Goldie, who was furiously sewing fresh white feathers on the skirt of her dress. Rosy noticed, though, that Goldie had kept three of the pearl strands on her gown and that they looked very stylish. "I'm just glad she hasn't shown her face again today. I don't know what I'd say to—"

"*Shh!*" said Rosy.

"Good after*noon*, Sylva," said Clara.

Sylva had appeared at the bottom of the stairs. I hardly need say how sorry she looked and how much sorrier she felt. Squeak held out her arms to Sylva, and Rosy came over and gave her a hug, which, to tell you the truth,

made her feel almost worse.

"I'm sorry I spoiled everything," said Sylva, "and ruined the ball." She had cried out almost all her tears, but there was one still left. It fell now.

Clara spoke up at once. "The ball is not

ruined, Sylva," she said. "And we've managed to salvage our gowns. The sea glass even looks quite nice." She smiled a small smile. Then her face turned serious. "We know you meant well"—Goldie raised an eyebrow—"but it's always a good idea to ask first."

"I know that now," said Sylva. "And I really am sorry."

"You're forgiven," said Clara and Rosy together. Goldie mumbled something that might have been "Fine," but no one could quite hear her.

"Shall I help you—"

"No, it's all right, Sylva," said Clara quickly. "We'll just slip our dresses on and fix our hair, and we'll see if the carriage is at the door."

Sylva sat in a corner of the great room and watched.

In next to no time, Clara had brushed out her long dark locks, Rosy had caught her coppery hair back with a simple pink comb, and Goldie had swept up her golden hair into a gorgeous pile of curls. She fastened a feathered tiara on the crown of her head. Rosy tied a couple of daisy-chain bracelets on her wrist, and Clara slipped a bright coral ring on her finger.

There was a whirring sound outside the door.

"I hear the carriage coming!" cried Goldie.

I suppose you are thinking the fairies were taken to the ball in a carriage drawn by snow-white horses or jet-black steeds or even a pair of loyal drays. But fairy carriages are not a bit like our carriages! They are made of oyster shells that have been polished to a high gloss silver by the Curricle sisters, who know how to do such things. Inside, they're lined with the softest milkweed down and furnished with pussy-willow cushions. And fairy carriages are pulled by a team of six matching dragonflies: That's why they make a buzzing sound.

The Fairy Bell sisters—all except Sylva—could not have been more excited. "It's time!" said Goldie. "How do I look?"

"You look elegant and beautiful," said Rosy.

"I suppose I do look quite elegant and beautiful," said Goldie. "Now, shall we go?"

Goldie started out the door without so much as a glance at Sylva.

"Aren't you forgetting something?" asked Clara.

"Bye, Sylva," Goldie muttered.

"That too," said Clara. "But you're forgetting the most important thing: We need to take off our wings."

That's another thing most children—the children who are not reading this book, for instance—do not know about fairies: Their wings come off. Like anything else, wings need cleaning and repairing from time to time, so they slip on and off for ease of care. Once a year, however, ordinary fairy wings are replaced by special wings, which are given to each fairy at the Fairy Ball.

"Oh, of course!" said Rosy. "Sylva, can you look after our wings for us?"

"You aren't going to let her—"

"Hush, Goldie," said Clara. She looked at Sylva and shook her head. "No touching, Sylva. And no leaving the house until we are home."

"Will you do us the honor of looking after

our wings?" said Rosy.

"I will," Sylva said. "I will do all that you expect of me."

Clara, Rosy, and Goldie doffed their wings and laid them out on the round copper wing table. Rosy patted hers gently.

"Ready?" asked Clara.

All four Fairy Bell sisters—and Squeak in Sylva's arms—joined in a circle around the wing table. They had the clearest voices on all of Sheepskerry Island, and they sang out bright and true. First they sang all together,

Keep our wings safe from harm
With this heartfelt fairy charm.
A circle, a circle.

Then they sang the song again as a round, with Clara beginning, Rosy joining in, and then

Goldie and Sylva adding their voices, until they reached the last line, all together.

A circle, a circle.

"Woo-woo!" said Squeak.

"Yes, it is beautiful," said Goldie. "We sound just like bells ringing. And we stayed on key, even though Tink was not here to lead us!"

The dragonflies' whirring got louder. "We must be off," said Clara. "Bye-bye, sweet Sylva. Tomorrow is *your* special day."

Sylva had almost forgotten about her birthday. She brightened up a little bit.

"And next year you will be at the Fairy Ball!"

That cheered her up even more. Rosy gave her a tight hug. "Thank you for trying so hard, Sylva," she said in a whisper.

"You look beautiful, Rosy," said Sylva.

"Happy almost birthday," said Goldie. "Don't have any more bright ideas."

And with that, the three sisters picked up their evening bags, slipped on their dancing shoes, crowded into the carriage, and were flown off to the ball.

The drone of the dragonflies' wings seemed to take a very long time to fade.

"*Squeak!*" said Squeak, just as she had the night before. Sylva shivered.

"Nonsense, Squeak," said Sylva. "That's the carriages going by. Nothing more." But Sylva held Squeak tight.

I'm not happy to say it, but now might be a good time to tell you more about trolls. You'll already know that trolls are jealous and grumpy creatures, who live under bridges and among the toadstools and bracken of the forest. They're too big and lumbering to fly, so they envy Queen Mab's powerful magic and wish they had some fairy magic of their own.

I imagine you're wondering why Clara and Rosy and Goldie would leave their sisters alone when trolls are about, but don't be worried: Fairy houses are protected by magic, and

it would take ten trolls—or more!—all work-
ing together to get through the birch-twig door.
And everyone knows that trolls don't like to
work together on anything.

fifteen

"No lolo," said Squeak.

"Oh, I'm not sad," said Sylva. "Not anymore." She had slept almost all day long, so she was full of energy now at dusk. The Bell fairy house was mostly neat and clean, but there were a few hairpins on the moss floor, and there were always a few sticks and twigs out of place, so Sylva had a bit of a tidy up, played a game of fairy peek-a-boo with Squeak, and then settled down to read.

She was just about at the part where the princess slayed the dragon when she heard a rumbling beneath the great-room floor.

BRUUMMMMM. BRUMM.

"Squeak!" said Squeak.

"Hush, Squeak. It's nothing," said Sylva, more sharply than she meant to. "Thunder, maybe?" But she drew her fairy blanket up close to her as she kept reading.

Not two pages later, when the princess had scaled the wall of the castle, the rumbling came again.

BRUMMMMM.

And again.

BRUMM. BRUMM.

"Oh no!" said Sylva in a whisper. "Squeak, I've tried to think it was something else. But now we have to face it. It's the trolls, Squeak. The trolls are coming. And we're all alone!"

Sylva peered out the window. She saw exactly what she was expecting: nothing at all. Trolls, as you know, travel underground, in tunnels, so their passage cannot be seen. But Sylva had spent enough time in Troll Tracking at Fairy School to know that trolls left clues as to where they were.

"Oh, Squeak," said Sylva. "Is that a crack in the grass?"

It was.

"And are those roots coming up a bit more than they should?"

They were.

"And—oh my!—has a whole branch snapped off the spruce tree?"

It had.

Sylva took Squeak in her arms. There had to be a lot of trolls to leave this many signs. "Don't worry, little one. The trolls are meanies, but our magic is more powerful than theirs. They can't get past our birch-twig door no matter how hard they try."

At least she hoped not. Sylva wasn't actually sure *what* this many trolls could do. Trolls almost never pooled their magic together—unlike fairies, who often helped and shared. But if the trolls did join forces, if they wanted something so much they would put their differences aside—

"Oh, Squeak! Who could say what such powerful ancient magic could do!"

Sylva knelt down and put her hand on the

soft moss just inside their door. She was listening and feeling for the trolls, not looking for them.

Brrrruummmm. Brummm.

The vibrations under the ground were getting fainter and farther away.

"They're not heading this way," said Sylva. "But where *are* they heading?"

She put her ear to the ground to listen harder. She had a suspicion she knew where the trolls were going to wreak their mischief and meanness. She hoped very much she was wrong.

But she could feel it.

The vibrations led past the Bell fairy house . . .

. . . around Deepwater Spring . . .

. . . alongside Cathedral Pines . . .

. . . and deep into the Windswept Gardens.

Which meant the trolls would soon be right under—

"Queen Mab's palace!" Sylva caught her

breath. "But why so many of them? And why tonight?"

Moonlight lit up Squeak's fairy crib, and Squeak squeaked again.

"Oh no!" cried Sylva. She could barely say the words. "The trolls want to steal the Narwhal's Tusk!"

Sixteen

Sylva did not know what to do. Queen Mab's orchestra of hummingbirds and pumpkin drums and honeybees would be far too loud for the fairies to hear the trolls' thrumming. And if they couldn't hear the trolls coming, they might turn their backs on the Narwhal's Tusk. Even a moment of inattention could spell disaster.

"A-nan-na!" said Squeak.

"You're right!" said Sylva. "We've got to save the Narwhal's Tusk. We have to tell Queen Mab. But how will we do it? All the older fairies are at the ball, and just the littlest sisters are left behind. Oh, Squeak, whatever will we do?"

Even as far away as Sylva was, she could still feel the faint rumble of the trolls as they tunneled to the palace. She had to get there, and quickly.

Just then there was a knock at the door.

"Who is it?" said Sylva. Everything seemed a bit scary now.

"Sylva, it's me. Poppy!" called a familiar voice.

"Oh, Poppy! I'm so glad it's you," said Sylva as she opened the door. "Did you hear it, too?"

"I did!" said Poppy. "That rumbling and brummmbling. Is it what I think it is?"

"Yes, it must be the trolls," said Sylva. "And they want—"

"—the Narwhal's Tusk!"

The two best friends caught their breath for a moment. Then Sylva said, "We've got to stop them. And I think I know how."

Seventeen

When she thought back on it later, Sylva couldn't have said how she had the courage to approach the copper wing table. She couldn't tell how she put on all three extra sets of wings—Clara's, Rosy's, even Goldie's—to give her the power she knew she'd need to get to the palace in time to stop the trolls. Somehow she did it. Would harm befall her doing precisely what she'd told her sisters she would not do? She couldn't think about that now.

She only thought about the fairies at the Fairy Ball. If the trolls got hold of the Narwhal's

Tusk, all its magic would go to them. Sylva shuddered as she pictured how the trolls would laugh as her sisters' beautiful diamond wings transformed back to moonlight at the Chief Troll's touch. The fairies would not be able to catch the trolls, as they'd be wingless! The ball would be ruined. And, worst of all, Queen Mab would lose her most powerful magic.

"You look after Squeak, Poppy," said Sylva. "I'm going out to save the ball."

"Do you really think you can do it, Sylva?"

asked Poppy. But Sylva had already sped away. "Good luck, Sylva!" Poppy called after her. "Be careful!"

Sylva had never flown so fast. She knew she'd have the force of four sets of wings to speed her journey, but there was something more. It was as if the spirits of her sisters were there on her shoulders—the wisdom of Clara, the kindness of Rosy, the confidence of Goldie—giving her more strength and power.

The question was: Would it be enough?

eighteen

Sylva was at Queen Mab's palace in an instant. The brummmbling of the trolls had stopped. All was quiet and calm. Could she have been wrong? What if she flew into the ball, in her sisters' borrowed wings, and told Queen Mab there would be a troll attack—when it was perhaps nothing more than thunder all along? She didn't dare. Not till she was perfectly sure.

Sylva peeked in the window. "Oh my!" she said in a whisper.

A long golden hall of gleaming glass and glowing candles, jewels, and polished stone opened up before her. Queen Mab's orchestra played the most enchanting music. There was the petting zoo in one corner! And cupcakes piled high in another. There were loads of presents! And, oh, the fairies' gowns!

Every fairy on Sheepskerry was dressed in her greatest finery.

"There are Poppy's sisters!" said Sylva to herself. "I will have to tell Poppy how beautiful they look!" Iris Flower was in purple, of course; Susan was in wild orange, to show off her deep black eyes; and Daisy was in Swiss dot, looking like a summer meadow. The Oak sisters, Acorn and Seed, looked so elegant in their rustling brown gowns with their pretty caps. The Seaside sisters were there, too, in shades of blue, aqua, and gray-green. How lovely they all looked. But where were the Bell girls? Where were the Fairy Bell sisters?

At last Sylva caught sight of them.

If her sisters' gowns had looked beautiful at the Bell fairy house, they looked absolutely breathtaking inside Queen Mab's palace. Clara's turquoise silk glistened in the candlelight, with Sylva's chips of sea glass catching the most light of all. Rosy was beautiful in her sweet pink gingham, which matched the glow in her cheeks. And Golden was, of course, simply perfect, the most stylish young fairy there by far.

Sylva cast her eye around the ballroom again. Something was missing, but what was it?

Wings! None of the fairies had wings!

Just then, the orchestra stopped playing. A single trumpet fanfare burst forth. Queen Mab was about to speak. Sylva thought she felt a tiny rumble, but she couldn't be sure. Did she dare interrupt the ball at the most important moment of all?

"Welcome to the Fairy Ball!" Queen Mab proclaimed, with a wide smile. "Tonight, you came to me wingless. Now I will reward your trust with the Gift of the Season. Beware: You will feel the chill of moonlight for a moment while I work my magic. Then you will dance with wings of diamonds."

Join your hands and hold your breath,
Spirits come from deepest depth,
    By Narwhal's Tusk and our own might,
    Wings: Transform from brightest light!
Replace our wings of every day.
Shine and sparkle! Wings away!

Sylva held her breath. At that moment icy moonlight fell on the fairies' shoulders and turned into wings of diamonds.

There was a gasp as the fairies looked around at one another.

"Oh, Queen Mab! Thank you!"

"They're *incredible!*"

"I've never
seen anything so
amazing in my life!"

"Can I keep them?"
(Was that Goldie?)

The new wings sparkled in
the light and threw off rainbows of
color on the windows and walls. Diamond wings
moved differently from regular wings—slower,
more gracefully—and they looked almost as glorious folded up as they did spread out for flight.
Sylva could have watched all night.

But even as the fairies spread their new wings, there was a very faint rumbling and a brummmbling from underneath the palace. It jolted Sylva back to attention. This time there was no mistake. The trolls had chosen their moment well!

nineteen

It all happened in an instant.

One moment, the fairies were dancing the Dance of the Diamonds.

The next moment: TROLLS!

Big, nasty, hairy, smelly trolls tumbled into the delicate Fairy Ball. They trampled the satin ribbons. They smashed the mirrors. They broke the chairs and frightened the animals. And the Chief Troll had his grubby paw on the Narwhal's Tusk.

The fairies' frightened voices rang through the ballroom.

"Stop them!"

But it was so hard to fly with the heavy diamond wings on their backs.

"Tackle them!"

But it was not easy to move in the elegant gowns.

"Run them down!"

But the fairies' dancing slippers were not made for running.

And even worse, the diamond wings were disappearing. They were turning back into moonlight, and the moonlight was fading away.

This was Sylva's moment.

She flew in through the high window with the power of her four sets of wings.

"I'll save the Narwhal's Tusk!" she cried.

twenty

Sylva swooped over the ballroom. She was tiny and she was young, but she had one great advantage: She was the only one in the whole assembly who could fly. The Narwhal's Tusk was what the trolls wanted, and the fact that the Chief Troll had it in his warty hands meant that Queen Mab's power was sorely depleted.

"I'm coming!" cried Sylva.

The fairies were doing their best to save the ball. It was most important to shield the animals in the petting zoo, so they gathered in a circle around the frightened pets and tried to calm

their fears. The cupcake tower had of course been demolished by the greedy trolls, and the presents were all stolen. The ball was spoiled. But that didn't matter. What mattered was to save Queen Mab's magic.

The one place the trolls were not looking was *up*. Suddenly Sylva heard a gasp.

"Is that . . . *Sylva*?"

"What is she doing here?"

"She's not old enough!"

"She's in danger!"

Clara, Rosy, and Goldie had spotted their sister.

"She has my wings!"

"Hush," said Clara. "She has our wings so she can save us all."

"Go, Sylva, go," said Rosy under her breath.

The Chief Troll was turning to address the crowd. He had the Narwhal's Tusk grasped tightly in his damp hand. He laughed a very mean laugh.

"Magic gone. Trolls take!"

"Not so fast!" cried Sylva.

She swooped down from her perch on the crystal chandelier. She hovered for an instant over the Chief Troll's head. Then she made a grab for the Narwhal's Tusk.

"Give that to *me!*"

"Huh?" said the chief. His reflexes were slow, as he was a troll, but he sensed enough danger to clutch the tusk to his chest. "Magic mine!"

"That's not yours—that's Queen Mab's!" And fiercely she grabbed onto the tusk. Would she wrest it free?

Aha! For once it came in handy that trolls were such sweaty creatures, because the Narwhal's Tusk was easy to slip out of the Chief Troll's fist.

"Wha?" said the Chief Troll.

"I've got it!" she cried.

But she didn't need to say a word. The moment the tusk was back in fairy hands, Queen Mab's magic began to surge back. The candles relit themselves. The mirrors gleamed once more.

"Quick, Sylva! To Queen Mab!"

Clara's wise words were exactly what Sylva needed to hear to clear her mind. She darted to Queen Mab and put the tusk safely back in her hands.

"I'll speak with you later, my child," said Queen Mab quickly. Then she turned her attention to the task at hand.

"Trolls, begone!" she cried, and the room filled up with the sound of her voice. "Fairies, restore!" And with that, the fairies' wings transformed into their diamond glory, and as Rosy told her later, their wings surged with power.

As if they had planned it, the fairies moved all together to rout the trolls from Queen Mab's palace. The Shepherd sisters herded the hairy creatures out the south door. The Flowers pushed them through the soft soil of the rose beds down to the tunnels where they belonged. And the Bell sisters crowded around Sylva.

"Oh, Sylva! How did you know about the trolls?"

"How brave you are!"

"Is someone looking after Squeak?"

"You're at the Fairy Ball and you're not even eight years old!"

Sylva was panting and out of breath from her daring rescue. She was just about to speak when she heard Queen Mab's commanding voice as the clock tower of the fairy palace began to toll the hour.

"Sylva Bell. Come before the fairy throne at once."

twenty-one

Sylva felt instinctively that a young fairy should never address the queen directly. But she couldn't help herself. "Oh, great queen," she said. "I would never have intruded on the ball if it hadn't been for the tro—"

"Hush!" said Queen Mab's attendant, Lady Courtney. "Queen Mab speaks first."

"But I just—"

"Quiet, I say!" said Lady Courtney. "Queen Mab speaks first *always*."

"Thank you, Lady Courtney," said Queen Mab. "But we don't use those rules so much anymore." Then she turned to Sylva, whose four sets of wings quivered. How would the queen punish her for entering the ball without an invitation, and before she was old enough to be there?

"Sylva Bell," said Queen Mab gently. "You alone recognized the trolls' danger. You alone came up with a plan. And you alone had the courage to save us all from great and lasting peril."

"She did beautifully!" came a whispered voice from the crowd. Sylva wasn't sure, but she thought it might have been Goldie.

"But I shouldn't be here," said Sylva sadly. "I'm not eight fairy years old."

The clock in the fairy palace tolled the last chime of midnight. Sylva had hardly ever been up so late. "I suppose I should go back home, my queen, and help my best friend, Poppy, look after little Squeak."

Queen Mab took Sylva Bell's downcast face in her hands. She tilted her chin up so she could

look straight into Sylva's eyes.

"Sylva Bell, sister of Tinker, Clara, Rosy, Golden, and Euphemia Bell"—for that was Squeak's real name—"it is now past midnight, and you are eight fairy years old. Now you are welcome to stay at the Fairy Ball."

A great cheer went up from all the fairies. Queen Mab allowed the cheer to go for a full two minutes; then she said, "Quiet, fairies, please.

"Sylva Bell taught us three lessons tonight," she said. "She taught us that it is good to take risks. Sylva took a great risk in wearing her sisters' wings and believing she could defeat a troop of trolls."

The fairies nodded in agreement, especially those who were still sweeping up after the trolls' mess.

"The second lesson Sylva taught us, including me," said Queen Mab, "is that perhaps our love of shiny things has made us imprudent."

"Imprudent?" whispered Goldie.

"It means," said Queen Mab, "that we could be a bit more sensible at our next ball. We all love elegant dresses and dancing slippers, but we should always make sure we can run in our shoes and move in our gowns."

"*Humph*," said Goldie, but very quietly.

"And the final lesson I've learned from Sylva is that the Fairy Ball should be for *all* fairies,

young and old. Next year, every fairy will be invited to the ball. The queen's fairy palace belongs to all of us."

This time, the cheer was louder than ever.

Queen Mab gently touched Sylva's four sets of wings with the Narwhal's Tusk. They transformed into diamonds, and Sylva felt power surge inside her. Then the queen waved the tusk over Sylva from head to toe. Sylva's everyday clothes turned into a radiant ball gown, complete with comfortable shoes.

"Go, my child. Enjoy the ball with my fairy blessing."

"Thank you, my queen!" said Sylva. And even Lady Courtney smiled.

With that, the music started up again, the chandeliers sparkled, and the fairies took their places for the Farewell Dance, with Sylva at the center of them all.

twenty-two

Other than being wing-weary from all that flying, and a tiny bit footsore from all that dancing, Sylva woke up the next morning feeling happier than she'd ever been in her life. If she hadn't seen her magnificent forest green gown in a corner of her room, she might have thought it had all been a dream.

"Wake up, sleepyhead!" Sylva heard Clara's voice calling her from downstairs. "We have a surprise for you."

Sylva sprang out of bed. Of course! It was her birthday. She pulled on her fairy slippers and hurried downstairs.

"Happy birthday!" cried her sisters.

They stood in front of a table with a most delicious fairy breakfast laid out before them. Not only were there chocolate scones and buttercup muffins, fruit and flowers, juice and jams and jellies—there was also a towering cake, eight layers high.

"Blueberry layer cake," said Clara.

"Made Sylva-style," said Goldie.

"One layer for each fairy year!" said Rosy.

There was a knock at the door. It was Poppy.

"Happy birthday, Sylva!" she cried. The two best friends shared a big hug. "Now we *all* get to go to the Fairy Ball this winter, thanks to you!"

"Sylva!" cried Golden. "Here's a note from Tink."

Happy birthday, darling Sylva!
News of your bravery has already reached us in Neverland.
Even Peter Pan is impressed!
See you soon, I hope.

xox
Tink

Sylva could not have been happier. Or so she thought.

A messenger dragonfly appeared at the

window. It was bearing a tiny gift.

"Look!" said Golden. "This is a present from Queen Mab herself!"

Sylva looked at the tiny box, which was beautifully wrapped in creamy water-silk with ribbons of deep-blue satin. The message on the card was simple and elegant:

For Sylva, for taking a risk.

Sylva slowly opened the box.

"What can it be?" asked Rosy. Even Goldie was in awe.

Sylva unfolded the soft velvet. Inside was a necklace with a golden chain. And at the end of the chain was—

"The Narwhal's Tusk!"

It was a tiny replica of the magical tusk she had saved last night.

"Queen Mab means you to wear this on

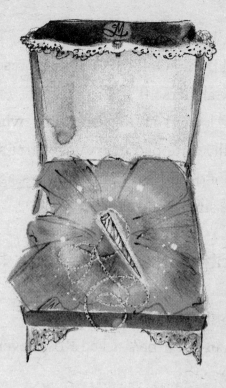

special occasions," said Clara. "It is a high, high honor."

Rosy put the necklace around Sylva's slender neck.

"It looks beautiful," said Goldie. "But more than that, you deserve it."

"Oh, thank you, Queen Mab! And thank

you, Goldie and Rosy and Clara and Squeak and Poppy! You are the best sisters and best friend a fairy could ever have."

"Bo-bo!" said Squeak.

"Yes, let's eat!" said Sylva. They all sat down to a glorious birthday breakfast, and laughed and talked and laughed some more about how Sylva saved the Fairy Ball.

fairy secrets

Squeak's Words

A-dah!: Perfect!

A-nan-na: Do something

Apa: More

Bo-bo!: Let's eat!

Coomada: Love it!

Doo: Pretty

No lolo: Don't be sad

Squeak!: Oops! or Uh-oh!
or Yay! or sometimes, Yikes!

Woo-woo: Beautiful

Sylva's Blueberry Birthday Cake

Sylva's birthday cake is easy and quick to make, especially if you don't separate the eggs. **Ask a grown-up to help,** and start by washing your hands.

Stoke a fairy oven with plenty of wood to make a glowing fire. If you don't have a fairy oven, use a regular oven. It should work almost as well. Preheat it to 350 degrees.

Mix together:

    1½ *cups flour* (sifted, if you enjoy sifting)

    1 *teaspoon baking powder*

    1 *teaspoon salt*

In a separate bowl, cream together:

    1 *cup sugar*

    ½ *cup butter* (Clara likes to use the unsalted kind)

    2 *eggs* (not separated! but no shells)

    1 *teaspoon vanilla*

Add the dry mixture to the creamed mixture alternately with:

    ½ *cup whole milk*

("Alternately" means that you mix a scoopful of the flour mixture into the creamed mixture. Then you mix in a good splash of milk, then another scoopful of flour mixture, then milk, and so on, till it all turns into a creamy cake batter.)

Next, gently fold in:
    1½ cups fresh blueberries, which you have sprinkled with
    1 *tablespoon flour*

Don't mix the batter too hard, or you'll bruise the poor berries!

Pour the batter into a buttered pan that measures 9 inches by 9 inches. If you don't have a square pan, a round pan does nicely, too.

If you want to get very fancy with your cake, you can add a topping before you bake it.

Here's how to make the topping.

Mix together:
   ½ cup light brown sugar
   ¼ cup flour
   3 tablespoons butter (unsalted again,
   says Clara)
   1 teaspoon cinnamon

When the mixture is crumbly, toss it over the cake batter. Make sure it gets into the corners, too. Then bake the cake in a fairy oven until it's done.

If you don't have a fairy oven, bake the cake 25–30 minutes (using regular minutes, not fairy minutes), and it should turn out perfectly.

The Bell Sisters' Wing Charm Song

To be sung as a round in three parts, to the tune of "Orleans, Beaugency"

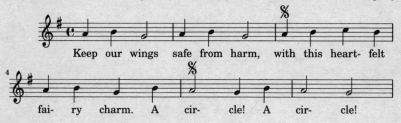

Keep our wings safe from harm, with this heart- felt

fai- ry charm. A cir- cle! A cir- cle!

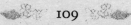

An excerpt from

Rosy
and the
Secret Friend

The Fairy Bell Sisters

Book 2

Rosy looked over at the fireplace mantel in their great room. There was a tiny seashell, painted bright pink.

"That was a gift from a long-ago Summer Child," said Rosy. "She gave it to Tinker Bell, or at least that's how the story goes." No one was quite sure whether that was true, but they liked to believe it was.

"The Summer Children's greatest gift was the Fairy Village in Cathedral Pines," said Clara.

"Pah-pah!" said Squeak.

"Yes, Squeakie. It *is* rather amazing. Summer Children built our fairy houses, one for every family of fairy sisters who live on Sheepskerry. And it's those houses we live in to this very day."

The sisters paused to think about those long-ago days. Their thoughts were interrupted by a clattering din coming from the dock, where the Summer People were arriving on the ferry. Goldie peered out the window. "Now the Summer People are horrible," she said. "They're especially horrible on Moving-In Day. We'll be trapped in this hot house till nightfall because of them."

"I'm sure they don't mean to be so thoughtless," said Rosy.

"I'm sure they do," said Goldie. "They spoil everything, every year." And she put her cards down. "It's no use," she said. "I can't concentrate with all this noise. Let's hide up in Tall Birch and watch them."

The Summer People were unloading the ferry and carrying all their many possessions up the boardwalks to the cottages. It took a long time, as Sheepskerry Island had no roads and no horrible metal monsters ("They're called 'automobiles,'" said Clara), and the Summer People filled up wheelbarrows to bring their boxes and bags, trunks and trinkets, to the cottages on the island. Sylva flew up to a lookout post. "Looks like there are five families this year, so one cottage will be empty," she called down to her sisters. "That's a relief."

"Wuh!" said Squeak.

"Yes, I'd love to do something about it, Squeakie," said Rosy. "But there's nothing we can do. We must just put up with them as best we can. Five families is an awful lot." She sighed. "But I suppose it's better than six. Be careful up there, Sylva!"

"I wonder why they need to bring so much stuff."

"And why must they make such a racket?"

asked Goldie. "Don't they know how sensitive
we are?"

"Come down at once, Sylva," called Clara.
"You mustn't be seen."

"Just one more minute—"

"Now, Sylva," said Rosy.

Sylva flew down from the birch as her sister

told her. "I wouldn't mind flying into a cottage while they're in there, just to see what the cottages are like when the Summer People are inside them," she said. "I could sneak up on——"

"Oh dear me, no," said Rosy, as crossly as she knew how (which wasn't very crossly at all). "You mustn't do anything like that. The Summer People are to be kept away from at all costs."

"Rosy's quite right," said Golden. "If these human people were to see our magic and discover that fairies live here, they'd tell all their friends, who'd come hunt for us with those telescope things——"

"Cameras."

"Yes, with cameras and torches and rakes and goodness knows what else. And that will be the end of us."

"But if we——"

"Hush, Sylva, that's enough," said Clara in a clipped tone. "You remember what happened on Coombe Meadow Island, don't you?" Clara didn't like to have to bring up faraway Coombe Meadow, but she had to stop Sylva's wild ideas.

The other sisters, even Squeak, fell silent. "Did all the fairies lose their homes?" asked Sylva at last.

"Every one of them. Their houses were trampled, their school was dug up, their queen's palace was destroyed—" Rosy had to stop for breath.

"—and many of them were chased till they dropped from exhaustion. So it is lucky that they all escaped." Clara didn't add "with their lives." She didn't need to.

"I thought Summer People were nice to fairies," said Sylva.

"Oh, they used to be nice to fairies," said Clara. "When children still believed in fairies." She sighed. "But those children don't exist anymore."

(How I wish Clara knew about you!)

"So if we value our homes and our lives and Sheepskerry Island, we must stay far away."

"Still, if I was very careful—"

"Sylva, I won't tell you again. You are not to go near a Summer Cottage or a Summer Dog or a Summer Cat or any of the Summer People. It is simply too dangerous. Do you understand?"

Sylva's eyes welled up.

"Sylva understands now," said Rosy gently to Clara. She hated to see Sylva so upset. "Don't you, Sylva?"

"I guess so."

"Good," said Rosy. "Then we'll all be safe."

It did not occur to Rosy then, or for a long time afterward, that it might be she who would trespass into the world of the Summer People.

Meet the Fairy Bell Sisters!

And look for more magical adventures coming soon!